Captured Prey
A Primal Play Novella
Reno R. Mist

POSH PANGOLIN PUBLISHERS

Captured Prey, A Primal Play Novella

Please note that the story, all names, characters, and incidents portrayed in this production are fictitious. No identification with actual persons (living or deceased), places, buildings, and products is intended or should be inferred.

Every effort has been made to trace or contact all copyright holders. The publishers will be pleased to make good any omissions or rectify any mistakes brought to their attention at the earliest opportunity.

Copyright © 2026 by Reno R. Mist

First Edition: January 2026

Book Cover: Get Covers
Character Art on page 30 (ebook): Illustration by Martyna Szpil
Character Art on page 64 (ebook): Illustration by Keturah Rose
Editors: Heartfelt Editing and Ebb & Flow Editing

ISBN: 979-8-9989053-3-9 (Ebook)
ISBN: 979-8-9989053-6-0 (Paperback)
Library of Congress Control Number: 2025924563

For permission requests, contact PoshPangolinPublishers@gmail.com
For author information, please contact Reno.R.Mist@gmail.com or visit https://www.renormist.com

Contents

Mi Lectores

My readers

Hello my little depraved and chaotic *lectores*. I know exactly why you picked up this book and trust me, no judgment at all. If you're here to explore, experiment, or just indulge in a delicious fantasy, then welcome. I wrote this with as much unhinged glee as the Cheshire Cat savoring his cream, and I hope you enjoy every sinful page just as much.

Before we dive in, I want to make sure we're all on the same page about triggers and boundaries. Consent is key—not only in the story, but in the reading experience, too. You might be excited for some of the themes we're about to explore, but others may not. Remember, it is always valid to step back if anything hits too hard.

First warning: this is a short read. This story is the first in the *A Second Circle Entry* series, which are meant to entice and entertain while expanding upon the hidden the world of the masquerade of magic and supernaturals that serves as the backbone to my other series. With that said, I have taken creative liberties with the mythology and folklore referenced throughout. Additionally, while I am of Hispanic and Italian descent, any errors in language, spelling, or translation are entirely my own (I swore an oath never to throw friends or family under the bus).

Below you'll find a list of hard triggers and the kinks featured in the book. Consider this your heads-up and your safe word rolled into one.

Minor spoilers ahead!

Our story features a Slavic leshy monster and a gutsy academic mortal in a dual-POV romance with a tall, dark, and handsome ancient forest god who can shift into a tree. Our 35+ FMC sees the beauty in the beast as their one-night stand spirals into an implied HFN/HEA, complete with fear play without harm, voyeurism, primal chase-through-the-woods tension, and a predatory power dynamic rooted in consent. Expect spicy scenes involving impressive girth, two-handed oral, creative vine usage, antler "handlebars," a woodland dinner for two, a sex swing, edging, orgasm denial, and the kind of heat that lasts until they pass out. Themes of negotiated consent and boundaries, exhibitionism, and voyeurism are explored, and readers should be aware of the following trigger warnings: explicit sexual content, and strong language.

I would forever be grateful that if you notice the TW list is incomplete on anything that could be triggering for another reader, please visit me on my website with a note so can add it.

Now that we have that out of the way, please enjoy!

Glossary & Pronunciations

Lasciate ogne speranza, voi ch'entrate (Lah-shah-tay oh-nyeh speh-rahn-tsah, voy ken-trah-tay)
Abandon all hope, ye who enter here.

Leshy *(LEH-shee)*
A tutelary deity of the forest in Slavic folklore. Leshy are ancient woodland spirits, often depicted as guardians or

as guardians or tricksters who protect the natural world
and punish those who disrespect it.

Lahs *(LA-hs)*
A leshy of undetermined age; known to have many
titles, including but not limited to, *Les Pravedniy, Lord
of Leaves,* and *Father of Forests.*

Les Pravedniy / Les Pravedny *(less prah-VED-nee)*
Russian for *"Righteous One of the Forest."* A sacred
woodland guardian, often associated with justice, protection, or divine judgment.

Vědma *(VYED-mah)*
A powerful Slavic *wise woman* or *witch.*

Volkhv *(VOLK-khuv)*
A powerful Slavic priest-shaman, magician, and seer.

Pequeña profesora *(peh-KEH-nyah
proh-feh-SOH-rah)*
Spanish for *"small teacher."* Often used as a teasing or
affectionate nickname.

Palomita *(pah-loh-MEE-tah)*
Spanish for *"little bird," "dove,"* or *"pigeon,"* depend-
ing on the region. Colloquially, it can also mean *pop-
corn*—usually to humorous effect.

Mi corazón de roble *(mee koh-rah-SOHN deh
ROH-bleh)*
Spanish for *"my heart of oak."* A poetic expression im-
plying strength, endurance, and unwavering resolve.

Mi tesoro *(mee teh-SOH-roh)*
Spanish for *"my treasure."* Coincidentally—and not
without intention—it is how Asmodeus regards you.

Second Circle *(SEK-und SUR-kul)*
A realm inspired by Dante's *Inferno.* In this world,
the Second Circle is the Domain of Asmodeus, where
desire is given form and temptation becomes tangible.

Asmodeus *(az-MO-dee-us)*
One of the Nine (9) Sins embodied in this world, cur-
rently reigning as the Sin of Lust. His domain governs
desire, longing, and the dangerous pull of obsession.

Malacoda *(mah-lah-KOH-dah)*

Leader of the Malebranche demons and steward of the Oubliette during Asmodeus's absence. A calculating enforcer of infernal order.

Ciriatto *(chee-ree-AHT-toh)*

One of the Malebranche demons, known for cruelty, sharp wit, and unwavering loyalty to infernal command.

Lilith *(LIL-ith)*

An ancient female figure appearing across multiple mythologies. Often associated with independence, desire, darkness, and defiance, Lilith embodies forbidden knowledge and untamed feminine power.

Dedication

Not every book is meant to make you feel something—some are just boring as fuck. This one is not one of those. So go on... run wild through the woods, my delicious feral bunny, and have the time of your life.

Preface

In every city worth its salt, I have built an Oubliette.

For those poor mortals whom I have not invited to come play, my opulent nightclubs must appear as fantastical playgrounds for the rich. However, even to those fortunate few whom I have sent invitations to, once they are inside Oubliette's walls, they only see what they expect to see: beautiful people sharing intimate moments and expensive drinks in an exclusive club.

But for those of us who know better, *mi tesoro*? We understand that Oubliette serves merely as a gateway for something greater.

For it is here, deep beneath each of my nightclubs, where lies the heart of every Oubliette: my Second Circle. Behind a door inscribed with my good friend Dante's warning, exists a realm where fantasy becomes flesh and desire finds its truest expression.

My realm.

Each door within my Second Circle opens to a different world, shaped by the deepest hungers of those brave enough to sign their names in crimson ink. Here, shame holds no currency. Here, pleasure becomes both sacrament and salvation. Here, the forbidden becomes possible.

What follows, *mi tesoro*, is the story of one such contract, one such surrender, one such transformation.

Lasciate ogne speranza, voi ch'entrate.

Abandon all hope, ye who enter here.

Welcome to my Second Circle. I have been expecting you.

Chapter One

Arrival

“This is a terrible mistake,” Celia Campbell said aloud to an empty alleyway.

She pressed her fingertips against the iron door before her, its surface warm despite the freezing winter night. Her breath frosted out in tiny puffs. The alley held no sound except her breathing: sharp, controlled, the kind of measured inhale she'd perfected before delivering lectures on Gothic literature, Occult studies, or Slavic folklore to bored undergraduates.

She'd discovered the address from a footnote in an original copy of *Dictionnaire Infernal*; Jacques Collin de Plancy's famous nineteenth-century tome about demons. The thought that the footnote may have been handwritten by Collin de Plancy himself was tantalizing. Once she arrived, she was stunned to find a nightclub named Oubliette at the address; the same name of the gentleman's club referenced in *Dictionnaire Infernal*.

Exploring the club was academic curiosity, she'd told herself for months. It would serve as good research for her next book on desire and agency in Gothic fiction. Nothing more.

Liar.

She stood shivering as her finger found the doorbell before her rational mind could intervene. The sound that emerged was less of a ring than a purr, vibrating through the door and into her chilled bones.

The door opened smoothly. A figure, androgynous and beautiful in ways that made her forget to categorize, smiled as if they'd been expecting her for years.

"Dr. Campbell. Welcome to Oubliette."

She hadn't given her name. "I think there's been—"

"No mistake." They stepped aside, revealing warmth that beckoned like an embrace. "I've heard you've been circling us for months."

The interior stole her breath. Crimson silk pooled from the ceiling like spilled wine, while the velvet walls invited touch. Candlelight danced across surfaces that seemed to breathe; the flames reflected in impossible patterns along the polished marble floors. The air itself hummed with something she couldn't name but felt in the space between her ribs.

Patrons moved through shadows like beautiful predators. A woman in midnight lace traced circles on another woman's wrist while they whispered to one another. A man in nothing but perfectly tailored leather pants watched the room with eyes that promised careful ruin. Everyone here looked like they knew exactly what they wanted. What they were.

Celia did not belong.

The bartender appeared as she approached the ebony bar, an impossibly attractive man whose smile held too much hidden knowledge. "What can I pour for you?" He asked. His short, curly hair was the color of wheat, and he had a jawline like a chiseled brick.

"Water," she said with a touch of desperation. "Just water... please."

She was too nervous to ask for his name.

Perched on the edge of a barstool, her spine rigid, she catalogued details as if she were taking research notes: the way conversations flowed like honey around her, the textures that begged for the touch of fingers. Celia was unable to ignore how her body responded to the atmosphere, despite her attempts to maintain academic distance.

Why are you really here?

She knew. God help her, she knew.

"Water is wise." The accented voice of a man came from everywhere and nowhere, silk wrapped around smoke. "Clarity before choices, *palomita*."

Celia turned, and her rational mind, the part that wrote footnotes and cited sources, shut down.

The man stood beside her barstool as if he'd materialized from the shadows themselves: tall and muscular with dark caramel skin, and midnight black hair with tousled waves caressing his ears. His features belonged in a Renaissance painting depicting an angel before his fall.

His suit was immaculate, a matte black trimmed in dark crimson, tailored to perfection to his well-built frame. When he smiled, Celia glimpsed teeth sharp enough to be dangerous. He wore colored contacts that gave his eyes an impossible golden glow.

You are dreaming. Are you dreaming? You must be dreaming. A man like that would only talk to you in a dream.

"Oh, I'm not here to um... make any choices," she mumbled as she sipped on her water.

"Is that so?" he asked in an amused tone. "Then do tell me, what are you really here for?"

"I am academic research. I am *here for* academic research." Flustered and blushing, Celia's words tumbled out in a breathless rush. "Anthropological study of modern ritual spaces and their psychological impact on contemporary urban populations. Specifically, the intersection of... um, of—"

"Desire and worship?" He slid onto the adjacent stool without invitation, moving with fluid grace.

"Yes," she answered, surprised. "How did you know?"

He flashed her a sharp-toothed smile as he extended his hand. "It is a pleasure to meet you, Dr. Campbell. I am Asmodeus."

Of course you are.

Because normal people had names like David or Michael, not the literal Prince of Lust from demonology texts. She took his hand. "Celia Campbell, but you seem to know that already."

"How could I not, *palomita*? I loved your book," he said as he nodded to the bartender.

"You've read... Really?" Despite herself, she was shocked and flattered. "Most people would not read an academic examination on the intersection between religious iconography and erotic subtexts in Gothic art and literature… unless I assign it to them."

The bartender set down a wine glass filled with a red so dark it was black. Asmodeus took a sip before he said, "I am not most people."

He's playing you. There's no way he actually read your book.

Celia didn't know where the courage came from to say what she said next, as she was not a combative person by nature. "Well, *Mister Asmodeus*, if you actually read my book, what was your favorite part?"

Another sip of wine. Another flash of that sharp-tooth smile. She could have sworn that his golden eyes brightened.

Sweet mother of God, he is dangerously attractive.

"That is difficult to choose, *pequeña profesora*." His accent caressed each syllable as he said, "But I suppose it would have to be a tie between… how sacred spaces became vessels for repressed sexual expression, particularly through the veneration of martyred saints, the architecture of confession, and the ritualistic aspects of religious devotion that mirror erotic surrender. Or," He took another sip of wine before he continued, "the special attention you give to the paradoxical relationship between religious ecstasy and carnal desire as expressed through artistic mediums that ostensibly served to reinforce moral boundaries while simultaneously providing outlets for subversive expression."

Oh.

She realized she was staring with her mouth agape. "You actually read my book?"

"*Sí*, I actually read your book. I never lie, *palomita.*"

Embarrassed, Celia drank her water and looked around the club, trying not to stare at any of the barely dressed patrons. She should apologize to the man masquerading as the Prince of Lust. After all, she more or less called him a liar.

She turned to open her mouth, but he spoke first in a low purr. "Again, I ask, why are you *really* here?"

You were not prepared for this. This man is out of your league. Abort.

"I told you, I am here for academic research."

"Dr. Campbell, I strongly suspect *research* is not what truly brought you to my House."

Celia stared at him for a moment as his words registered. "Your House?"

"*Sí*. I am the proprietor here, among many other things. Now, tell me, why are you *here*?"

"Academ—"

"No, do not tell me the lie you told yourself that brought you here. You already told me what your mind wants you to believe." His leisurely tone held the cadence of someone accustomed to being obeyed.

"I don't—" Her voice cracked. Professional composure scattered like papers in the wind. "I am here for research. For a new book. I was preparing for—"

"Surrender." His smile was patient, knowing. "Preparing for the chase. Preparing to be caught."

Heat flooded her cheeks, and she squeezed her legs together. "I don't know what you're talking about. You don't understand."

"I understand more than you allow yourself to." He gestured to the space around them, to the people who pulsed with permission and pleasure. "Do you see them? They come to me broken by lies. Lies about what they *should* want. What they *should* feel. What they *should* be."

A woman at a corner table threw her head back in laughter, unashamed joy radiating from every line of her body. A couple at the far end of the bar touched each other with reverence, worshipping each other's bodies, as if the world would end if they stopped.

"Mortals teach themselves that desire is sin," Asmodeus continued, taking another sip. "But desire is truth. The most honest thing you possess. Denying it does not make you virtuous. It makes you hungry."

Celia's hands shook around her water glass. "I'm not—"

"You dream of running." His voice dropped to a velvet whisper. "Through forests that exist only in your mind. Your heart pounds, your legs burn, and *something* follows behind you. Something not entirely human. Something from those Slavic folktales you love so much. Something that will catch you. Use you. Take from you everything you pretend you do not want to give."

The glass slipped. Water splashed across the bar, soaking into wood that seemed to absorb it with a thirst.

"But in your dreams," he leaned closer, "you never truly run fast enough to escape. Do you, *palomita*?"

Her throat closed. Years of careful control, of professional distance, of pretending she was nothing but intellect and analysis; all of it crumbled under his gaze.

"I want to run." The confession tore from her chest like a sob. "I want to feel afraid. I want to be caught and…" Her voice broke on the words she'd never spoken aloud. "Used. But I need to know it's a game. That I'm always in control, even when I'm screaming."

Asmodeus smiled, slow and approving, as if she'd finally spoken her own name correctly.

"So you want ravishment, not violation. Fearplay without harm." He produced a parchment from the inside of his suit jacket. "This makes it possible. A contract that safeguards your limits. This gives you exactly what you crave while also offering you safety and control."

She stared at the words, the ink somehow still wet and unsmeared. She hadn't seen him write anything.

When did he draft this? The words swam before her eyes. Professional. Precise. Rules that were defined and clear.

The parchment radiated warmth as if it were alive, pulsing like a beating heart. Celia read the terms with the same careful attention she gave ancient texts in the university archives. Each clause spelled out precisely what would happen, what wouldn't, and the boundaries that would remain sacred even in surrender.

This is madness. You're going to sign a contract with... with what? A stranger? A demon? A hallucination?

Her academic mind cataloged all the reasons to run. Her body remembered all the years of denial.

"What exactly would I be agreeing to?" Her voice sounded strange to her own ears, husky and wanting.

Asmodeus traced one slender finger along the edge of the contract, not touching her but close enough that she felt the heat of him. "The contract ensures no harm can come to you beyond that which you desire, and that I cannot keep you beyond our agreed timeframe." His smile was a crescent moon on a cloudless night. "If you sign this contract, you agree to be hunted, *palomita*. To feel the exquisite terror of prey. And I ensure you will be caught and taken by the *thing* you secretly desire... all while respecting whatever boundaries you set."

The thing *you secretly desire*. "What I want to chase me," she said, "you can't give me. It isn't real. It's just—"

"A myth?" he asked. His luscious lips drank another slow sip of his blood-red wine while he stared at her. She felt as if his golden eyes were drinking her in with every moment. "I make myths real."

Celia's academic mind screamed warnings about deals with devils, while the carnal darkness she kept locked in a cage within herself rattled its bars.

It's just a consent form. This is like signing a waiver before skydiving.

But she knew that whatever *this* was, it felt a hell of a lot riskier than skydiving.

Asmodeus's voice reached into her heart and tugged as he said, "You will receive exactly what you have denied yourself, *pequeña profesora*. The chase. The capture. The sweet surrender that your mind craves but your pride rejects."

"And what will you receive?" The professor in her surfaced, analytical even now.

His laugh wrapped around her like silk sheets. "I feed on desire, *palomita*. On the moment when shame dissolves into honesty. On the pleasure that follows truth. And," he pointed to the bottom of the contract with a slender finger, "that is my final payment, which you will render upon fulfillment of your fantasy."

She read the line he pointed to, her brow furrowing. What in the hell? "I don't understand. You want a memory of mine?"

"*Si*. A trifle thing. And I would not be taking it away from you, *palomita*. I would simply make a copy of it for myself."

Celia's throat tightened. She'd spent her entire adult life building walls between her mind and body; between her public self and private hungers. It had taken years to curate the careful, precise professor who analyzed desire and sexuality in Gothic art, but who never admitted to experiencing it herself.

For some reason, she thought of her apartment: meticulously organized books, color-coded closet, a life built around control and predictability. She thought of all the nights alone with her erotic novels, her fingers between her thighs, imagining what it would feel like to be pursued, overwhelmed, *taken*.

"You already know what you want," Asmodeus said, his honeyed voice sending warmth to her core. "The only question is whether you will finally allow yourself to have it."

What would your colleagues think? What would your students say if they knew?

But here, in this place where candlelight kissed skin and secrets hung in the air like perfume, those questions felt hollow. No one here knew Dr. Campbell, the shy and silent professor nearing her forties. No one here cared about her publications or her professional reputation.

Her fingers trembled on the parchment. "I'm afraid."

"Of course you are, *palomita*." His voice softened. "Fear and desire live in the same house. They share the same bed."

"Let's say I do sign it, but then I change my mind?" The question tumbled out before she could stop it.

"That is what this is for." His finger traced her wrist, drawing lines of crimson fire across her skin. Where he touched, a rune appeared. It was luminous and warm. "Your emergency rune. Simply wish for it to activate, and you'll return here instantly. No matter how deep in the fantasy you fall."

The mark pulsed once, then settled into her skin as if it had always been there.

Do it, coward. We came here for this.

An ornate pen appeared in Asmodeus's hand, the nib gleaming gold. He offered it to her like a gift or a challenge.

"Your signature gives permission only to yourself, Celia. To be the woman who lives behind your eyes when you are alone in the dark."

She took the pen. Its weight felt right, felt inevitable.

"Chase me," she whispered, and signed her name.

Chapter Two

Descent

"Ready, *palomita*?"

Asmodeus extended his arm like a gentleman offering a stroll through a garden rather than a descent into temptation. Celia hooked her elbow through his, surprised by the warmth radiating through his suit jacket. Genuine warmth, real flesh, despite every rational part of her mind insisting he couldn't be what he claimed.

"What does that mean?" she asked, unsure if he would respond to her inquiry.

"I simply call you what you are. *Palomita*, my little dove. *Pequeña profesora*, my little professor. No offense meant. It is simply how I see you."

It feels almost... endearing, she thought as they moved through Oubliette's main floor toward a black marble staircase that curved down into shadows. The club hummed around them with whispered conversations and silk-soft laughter, but it felt distant now—background music to her own racing heartbeat.

You signed the contract. No turning back now.

"The contract," she said as their footsteps echoed against marble, "how did you write it?"

"With a pen and ink," Asmodeus said with a smirk.

"No, I mean... the clauses within the contract are perfect. Exactly as I would have written them, exactly what—"

"What you desired, *palomita*?"

Warmth flooded her face. "Yes."

How Asmodeus had known exactly what she wanted, exactly what she *needed* to give into this carnal fantasy, was a mystery. But the terms were clear: no actual pain, just primal force; to be chased until caught; to be taken; and to have complete and total control as to when to stop.

Assuming that glow-in-the-dark temporary tattoo he slapped on your wrist actually works.

She was compelled to ask, "This um… emergency rune, as you called it. How does it work?"

"*¿Nerviosa, pequeña profesora?*" His voice held amusement but no mockery. "That is good. Fear sharpens pleasure. But you need not worry on account of the rune. It *will* work, or else I shall carve out mine own heart and gift it to you as recompense."

The staircase spiraled down past the second level, past the third, into depths that seemed improbable. Each level they passed glowed with its own particular flavor of carnal pleasure: glimpses of rooms where beautiful people explored desires with artistic precision. The stairwell ended at a solid black iron door inscribed with the Italian phrase, "*Lasciate ogne speranza, voi ch'entrate.*" *Abandon all hope, ye who enter here.*

Celia stifled a laugh at how cheesy and cliché it seemed for the line from Dante's Inferno to be carved into the door of a sex dungeon. She asked, "Rather ominous for a house of pleasure, isn't it?"

"No. Not ominous," Asmodeus said as he waved a hand at the door. It opened on its own, creaking on thick iron hinges. "Within my House, desires are made manifest. There is no need for *hope* when you have certainty."

She nodded as she stepped through the threshold into a long hallway. There was a sudden gust of warm wind at her back, a heat that urged her forward. A corridor stretched ahead, illuminated with smokeless torches in iron sconces and lined with doors. Each door was different: some atavistic, heavy wood studded with iron, others sleek modern surfaces that reflected the torchlight like mirrors. Behind each one, Celia imagined, someone else's deepest fantasy played out.

How many people have walked this hallway? How many have signed contracts like yours?

Asmodeus fell in step beside her, the large door creaking closed behind them. "*Palomita*, your hunter will pursue with single-minded determination until you activate your rune. You may activate your rune at any time and for any reason. Do you understand?"

Her face felt hot. *Why does everything this man says sound so sexy?*

"I... yes. I understand."

"Good. Then your hunter will not stop until this lights up." He brushed his thumb across the rune on her wrist, making it flare with soft light.

They continued onward, the warm breeze occasionally rising to sharp gusts of wind despite the fact that they were deep underground. The walls along the hall were carved stone, no longer the silk-and-velvet luxury of the upper floors. They had passed countless doors recessed into those stone walls, each one made from a different material in a different style. No two doors appeared to be the same.

"Your hunter," Asmodeus said, "you are certain this is what you want?"

"Yes," she said without hesitation.

"Why a leshy?"

The question caught her off guard. She had spent so many hours lost in her fantasies, but she'd never thought to examine the reasons for her desires aloud, even to herself, and certainly never to another person. "I..." She swallowed hard. "I am unsure. I suppose..."

"Yes," Asmodeus prompted gently.

"I suppose I find them beautiful, in a savage... terrifying way."

"That," he said as he turned to look at her, "has been one of the most honest things you have said all evening, *pequeña profesora*."

She looked at him and said, "When it catches me..."

"*Sí?*"

"I want to be taken by a man. A beautiful man."

Asmodeus smiled, sharp teeth gleaming in torchlight. "Transformation. The beast becomes the beauty. Very romantic, *palomita*."

"It's not romantic," she protested, though her pulse quickened. "It's primal. Base. Nothing romantic about it."

"If you say so."

Asmodeus stopped in front of a door that looked like it belonged to a medieval castle: dark wood bound with iron, with a handle worn smooth by age and use. "Once you step inside, it will feel completely real. Your mind will know it's a fantasy, but your body will experience every sensation as if it were happening."

She stared at the door. Beyond it lay everything she'd dreamed of and been too ashamed to pursue. "How long will I be inside?"

"Until you are satiated." His golden eyes held hers. "Or until you wish for your rune to bring you out. Celia... is this what you want?" Asmodeus asked, his hand on the door handle.

No. Yes. I don't know.

But that was a lie. She did know. She'd known since she began her academic career in occult and folklore studies and first read about heroines fleeing through moonlit forests: pursued by dark figures who caught them, claimed them, and loved them despite their protests. She'd known every time she'd touched herself to fantasies of being overpowered, taken, used.

She'd known the moment she discovered rumors of this place from the dusty footnote of an academic text.

"This is what I want."

Asmodeus turned the handle. The door swung open on silent hinges.

Warm mist rolled out like breath on a cold morning. Not the sticky humid air of the club, nor the freezing winter chill from outside; this was comforting, fresh, and earthy. Through the doorway, Celia glimpsed trees; tall, dark shapes that stretched up toward a ceiling she couldn't see. Moonlight filtered through fog, painting everything silver.

How is this possible?

She stepped through the threshold. The scent of damp earth and growing things filled her nose. Real earth, real plants. The sound of wind through leaves whispered from the darkness beyond.

"How," she breathed, "is it actually a forest?"

She turned to ask Asmodeus how they'd built such a thing in the basement of a club, but the space behind her was empty.

No Asmodeus.

No doorway.

She was alone in the dark, in a forest, under a full moon, and surrounded by nothing but trees and fog.

Cool earth pressed against bare feet, soft and yielding between her toes. Celia looked down at herself and blinked. Gone were her gray slacks and pressed button-down. Instead, she wore nothing but a white slip that barely reached her thighs; torn at the hem, the fabric was so thin that moonlight rendered it nearly transparent.

How? When had she changed clothes? When had—

A growl rumbled through the forest. Low, distant, but unmistakably real.

Her breath caught. The fantasy had begun.

Fog rolled between ancient oaks and silver birches like living silk, transforming the forest into something from a Gothic novel. Moonlight spilled through the canopy in broken streams, creating pools of silver and shadow that shifted with each breath of wind. The trees rose impossibly tall around her, their branches intertwining overhead like cathedral arches.

Beautiful. Terrifying. Perfect.

Her heart hammered against her ribs with a mixture of fear and carnal hunger, a primal urge that had been locked away behind years of careful academic composure. This was what she'd dreamt of since she first discovered stories of heroines fleeing through moonlit forests: the hunt, the delicious and joyous fear of being prey.

Warmth surrounded her skin despite the winter chill she'd felt outside Oubliette. Here, the air held spring's sweet promise, caressing her bare arms and legs with invisible fingers. She shivered. Physics meant nothing in fantasyland, apparently. Good thing, too, since she'd completely forgotten to negotiate shoes into her contract, and the soft forest floor welcomed her bare feet with the give of moss and fallen leaves.

Another growl echoed through the trees, closer this time. Definitely closer.

He's coming for you.

Her body responded to the sound with a jolt of heat that started low in her belly and spread outward like wildfire. A laugh bubbled up from her throat, high and breathless. Not nervousness, but exhilaration. She'd spent years analyzing the psychology of the chase in Gothic literature, the symbolism of pursuit and capture, the transformation of fear into desire.

Now she was living it.

She took a step forward, then another, choosing her direction at random. The fog parted around her movement like water, creating momentary clearings before closing again in her wake. Each step sent warmth shooting up from the earth through her legs, as if the forest itself recognized what she needed.

Run. The word whispered through her mind with primal urgency. *Run, or he'll catch you.*

But wasn't that the point? To be caught? To be claimed?

The contradictory desires warred in her chest; the thirst for being chased battling against the hunger to be captured. Her academic mind tried to catalog the competing impulses, to understand the psychology at work, but her body had already made its choice.

She ran.

Tree branches whipped past as she plunged deeper into the forest, her slip catching on thorns that left tiny tears in the fabric. The fog seemed to guide her path, opening corridors between the trees while obscuring others. Her feet found purchase on roots and stones with impossible sureness, as if the forest conspired to help her flight.

Behind her, something large moved through the underbrush. Not clumsy. Deliberate. Controlled. Hunting.

Heat pooled between her thighs with each footfall. This was it. This was what she'd craved in every secret midnight fantasy, what she'd found in the pages of every dark romance she'd hidden behind academic texts; the thrill of being hunted by something powerful, something that wanted her with single-minded intensity.

Her breath came in short gasps that had nothing to do with exertion. Each gulp of air seemed to feed the fire building in her core. She could feel him back there: watching, waiting, letting her believe she might escape before he closed the distance. The game was as much about the chase as it was the capture.

How close is he?

She risked a glance over her shoulder and thought she caught a brief glimpse of a leshy between the trees: impossibly tall, impossibly muscular, bark instead of skin, moss and leaves in place of hair and beard.

That's impossible. Isn't it?

Even at this distance, she felt his attention like heat against her skin. Leshy or not, the knowledge that she was being watched, being desired, being *hunted*, sent electricity racing through her.

Her nipples hardened against the gossamer fabric of her slip. The silk rubbed against sensitive skin with each movement, a constant reminder of her body's arousal. She was wet already, trembling and slick with want.

The trees thinned ahead, revealing a clearing bathed in silver moonlight. She broke free of the forest's embrace and stumbled to a halt in the center of the open space, chest heaving, slip clinging to her soft curves dampened with perspiration.

The clearing was silent.

No wind, no rustling leaves, no distant growls. Just her own ragged breathing and the thunder of her pulse. She scanned the treeline, searching for a face among the trunks and branches.

He's here.

The certainty settled over her like a blanket. Somewhere at the edge of the trees surrounding the clearing, her hunter waited. Her leshy. Watching her stand exposed in the moonlight, her body outlined through transparent silk, her arousal obvious in the way she trembled, in the way moonlight glistened off her slick thighs.

Let him look. Let him see what he'd done to her with nothing more than the promise of pursuit. She was already his, and they both knew it. The only question was how long he'd make her wait before he claimed what was already given.

Another growl, louder now, rolled across the clearing like thunder.

Celia smiled in the darkness and ran.

Chapter Three

Hunt

L ahs stood motionless among the trees, watching the mortal woman tremble with desire and anticipation. She'd looked directly at him at one point, but he was as still and motionless as his immobile forest brethren. At a glance from that distance, he looked like a tree with a vaguely humanoid shape; an odd tree, but that's all. Just a tree. If he had been closer, and if she had looked more closely, she would have seen the truth.

She would have seen a leshy.

She would have seen a muscular figure carved from living wood, one who towered over any mortal man she'd ever known. She would have seen a beard of moss that framed his face and black antlers that crowned his head, erupting from a mane of autumn leaves. She would have seen arms that were thick, corded braids of branches, legs like trunks of oak, and the hardened bark that was his skin.

Lahs knew the sight of him would have terrified her, but that *was* the point.

As Lahs watched his prey stumble through the underbrush like a spooked bunny, he recalled Asmodeus presenting this contract to him earlier that morning. Lahs had been tending one of his gardens in his forest, listening to the dawn chorus of warblers, blackbirds, and chaffinches. He heard the thoughts of every tree, brush, and budding flower as clearly as he heard the birdsong.

Yet still, the Prince of Lust snuck up on him.

"A fine morning to be gardening, *Les Pravedniy*," Asmodeus's voice had come from behind him.

Lahs turned to find the demon seated cross-legged on a fallen log, dressed in an immaculate forest green suit. Asmodeus gave Lahs a too-wide, toothy grin, and his golden eyes outshone the dawn's light. He'd looked as out of place in Lahs's primordial forest as Lahs would have looked on the dance floor of Oubliette.

"You call upon me as the 'Righteous One of the Forest'? If you are addressing me with one of my favorite formal titles," Lahs said as he bent down to stroke the soft pink petals of his musk mallows, "then you must want something, Prince of Lust."

Asmodeus laughed and waved a hand. "Oh, *mi corazón de roble*, I am simply showing you respect while I am a visitor in your domain."

My heart of oak indeed, Lahs thought with a scoff. Asmodeus had his little nicknames for everyone.

Satisfied his garden was healthy, Lahs stood to tower over Asmodeus. "And you are visiting me here and paying me respect... *because* you must want something."

The demon let out a heavy sigh. "It seems we have known each other for far too long, old friend. Very well," he'd said as he rose from the fallen log and dusted off his pants, "we can forgo the formalities if you wish, Lahs. I have come for the favor you owe me."

Lahs nodded. "I assumed as much. It has been so long... I half-suspected you'd forgotten."

"No," Asmodeus said with a short laugh, "I never forget a debt to repay or a favor I'm owed. I was simply waiting for," he trailed off as if he were tasting for the right words, "the *perfect* favor to ask for."

"Well," Lahs gestured for Asmodeus to follow him as he walked deeper into the woods, "ask away."

The Prince of Lust walked beside him, forced to take two strides for every one of Lahs's. "I have a guest who will be arriving in the Second Circle tonight with a singular desire only you can fulfill."

Lahs did not break his stride as he pushed aside saplings and underbrush. "Tonight?"

"*Si.*" A smile curved the demon's perfectly shaped lips. "She has been circling us for months, too anxious to enter. But tonight she will finally work up the courage to knock on our door."

"You are certain?"

The Prince of Lust nodded as he said, "As certain as sunrise."

For the briefest of moments, Lahs had wondered how Asmodeus always knew. How he could predict the desires of others with such accuracy, how he could anticipate a person's behaviour before they themselves even knew what they were going to do. But questioning the Prince of Lust was pointless. During his many millennia of knowing Asmodeus, Lahs had never once seen him proven wrong about the desires of others.

Except for Lilith. Nobody, not even Lust itself, ever knows what that woman wants.

Instead of probing how he was so certain, Lahs instead asked, "And you are telling me... why?"

"Dear *corazón de roble*, I want you to prepare to give her *exactly* what she needs." Asmodeus handed him the contract, terms detailed with precision. "Study this. Learn her desires. Honor them."

Lahs gave the contract a cursory glance. "I have ample woodland spirits at my disposal. I shall have one of them hunt the human. I would—"

"No."

The refusal was said without anger or malice; that wasn't Asmodeus's way. He was not one to raise his voice or fume or demand. He simply stated what he wanted and then he *got* what he wanted.

Lahs said, "If not one of my own, then perhaps a member of your Malebranche—"

"Lahs, I want *you* to fulfil this contract; not one of my incubi, nor one of my raksha, nor *any* of my demonic underlings." Then the Prince of Lust stretched an arm up, reached over his head to cup Lahs's cheek in a slender-fingered hand. "*You.*"

Lahs remembered looking down at Asmodeus and wishing, not for the first time, that his immense size and otherworldly strength actually mattered.

It didn't.

If Asmodeus were nearly any other creature, Lahs would tear him limb from limb for daring to give him orders. To come into *his forest* and make demands of him. But the Prince of Lust was so far beyond anything Lahs could comprehend that the ancient leshy could only nod his head as he reluctantly said, "If that is what you desire."

Asmodeus's face lit up with a grin as he'd said, "It is! It is precisely what I desire. I believe this will work out well for both of you. Trust me, *mi corazón de roble*."

While Lahs did not believe *everything* the Prince of Lust ever told him, as the scent of his prey drew him from his memories into the present, he was glad that he had trusted Asmodeus in this.

Rosemary and vanilla, he mused. It was a clean, civilized smell that had no place in this primal realm. But beneath that was the musk of fear-sweat and the sharp, unmistakable tang of arousal; *her* arousal, dripping down her pale thighs as she stood exposed in the moonlight.

Lahs inhaled deeply from his concealment among the ancient oaks, letting her scent flood his senses. She was everything mortals pretended they weren't: wet, wanting, hungry for things they'd been taught to deny. Was it hypocrisy that her body's desire betrayed the same fear she sought? Her heartbeat drummed through the forest like music, fast and erratic and sweet.

Too easy.

He could take her now. Cross the distance between them in five strides, pin her against the nearest tree, entwine her in vines, and claim what the contract had already given him. Her struggles would be token at best. After all, she wanted this. She'd signed her name to ensure it, and now every breath she took screamed surrender.

But the terms of the contract Lahs was meant to fulfill were explicit. She wanted to be hunted and not simply captured. Wanted the chase, the fear, the delicious terror of prey that knows it cannot escape.

Movement in the clearing drew his attention. The woman, Celia, had started walking, picking her direction at random. Smart enough to move rather than freeze, but not experienced enough to choose terrain that favored escape. Not that it would matter. The forest belonged to him, every root and branch an extension of his will.

He tracked her movement with predatory focus, keeping pace through the undergrowth without a sound. It was easy to remain hidden while she stumbled like a startled bunny, all clumsy grace and desperate energy. Her torn slip caught on brambles, creating new tears that revealed glimpses of creamy skin beneath.

Beautiful.

The admission surprised him. Most mortals were little more than bags of malicious meat to him. Trespassers in his sacred groves. Defilers of his beloved woods and glades. But this one? There was something in the way she moved, the determined set of her shoulders despite her obvious fear, that caught his attention.

She wound her way deeper into the forest, away from the clearing where moonlight had painted her in silver, toward the dense shadows where predators belonged. Good. Let her think the darkness offered safety. Let her believe she could hide from what pursued her.

He gave her a head start, counting heartbeats while her footsteps faded. Then he moved.

The forest bent to his will as he ghosted between the trees. Branches parted without a sound; roots shifted to accommodate his passage. He was part of the realm, part of the forest.

Her trail was easy to follow: broken twigs, disturbed earth, the lingering wisp of her scent. He would need to tend to his broken brethren once the favor was paid and the contract fulfilled. She'd tried to mask her direction by doubling back once, clever girl, but terror made her clumsy. Her fear left signatures only a predator could read.

Where is my little bunny? Ah... there.

He caught sight of her through the trees, pressed against bark as if it could protect her from what hunted in the darkness. Moonlight filtered through the leaves to paint her in fragments: her pale shoulder, the curve of her breast, the rapid rise and fall of her chest.

His nostrils flared. She smelled of sex and submission, like every dark fantasy that mortals denied themselves. His growing cock throbbed, demanding release, demanding he claim what was his.

Not yet.

But soon. Very soon.

He let her see him.

Lahs stepped into a shaft of moonlight within her line of sight; they were only ten feet apart. She stared at him with her mouth agape as he drank in the sight of her. At a glance, she appeared to be a fragile and pale little thing. Her tattered slip hung off one slender shoulder. She trembled, clutching at her chest... but her tantalizing hazel eyes betrayed her.

Interesting. There's a furious and defiant hunger there.

He had to admire that. At least a little. He took one step towards her, and she jerked upright, breath catching in her throat. He felt the spike of her terror like morning dew on his tongue.

Perfect.

She ran.

He chased.

Fear poured off her in waves, sweet and intoxicating. But beneath her terror was the overwhelming scent of her arousal. The chase was working exactly as intended. Terror and desire fed each other in an endless loop, building toward the inevitable conclusion.

He imagined what would come. Her body writhing beneath his, crying out in pleasure as he took what she'd offered. His cock hardened at the thought, blood-sap rushing between his legs as predatory hunger merged with increasing sexual need.

Soon... but not too soon.

He slowed his pursuit, allowing her to gain some ground and put distance between them. He hoped she would harbor an illusion of escape, of victory, for he knew that would make catching her all the sweeter.

But not as sweet as her scent.

He hated himself for the thought, but it was true. Her scent had made his head swim, made primitive urges claw at his control. How long since he'd taken a mortal? Years? Decades? How long since he'd taken one who was willing to lie with him, as this Celia was? How long since the bog-wives of ancient *vědma* had thrown themselves at his feet?

He could not say, which said a lot. It made this hunt feel different... made it feel personal.

Wrong word.

Nothing about this was personal. She was a contract, nothing more. She was a long-overdue favor he owed to a friend. She was a name on a parchment, terms to be fulfilled with professional efficiency. The fact that her scent made his mouth water, that the sound of her frightened breathing sent lightning coursing through him? That was irrelevant.

Focus. Where is she?

She had paused beside a massive oak to catch her breath. The smell of her intensified; fear and arousal in equal measure, a cocktail that made his blood-sap sing. The urge to lunge, pin her down, root her in place, and claim what was already his by right was nearly overwhelming.

No pain, he reminded himself. *Just primal force. She wants to be overwhelmed, not broken.*

The distinction mattered, though he couldn't say why. Usually, the difference between those two states was trivial. Pain, pleasure, fear, ecstasy? All tools in an arsenal, all means to the same end. But her contract specified ravishment, not violation. Conquest, not destruction.

What is she doing, he wondered as he slowly shifted into a better position to see her. From between the shaded boughs, he watched her lean back against the trunk of the oak and run one hand down her body. There was a brief flicker of her warm pink tongue licking her lips, then a flash of pearly white teeth as she bit down on her bottom lip. Her hand slid between her legs.

By all the glades and all the groves, this woman is something else.

He held his breath as he watched her touch herself. She threw her head back against the tree, and her luscious dark hair snagged in the bark. He wished it were *him* grabbing a fistful of her hair.

She placed her other hand over her breast, pinching a dusky nipple through her slip. The hand between her legs began moving furiously, and the tiniest whimper escaped her lips. *Fuck, she is exquisite.*

He released his held breath and then inhaled the delicious smell of her arousal, sharp and crisp in the night air. Watching her, hearing her, and smelling her caused his cock to throb with such intensity it felt as if it would burst.

He wanted to devour her. He could already taste her in the night air, but he hungered to bury his face between those thighs, drive his tongue into her depths, and drink every drop as her screams shook the branches above. He reached down, took his cock in his hand, and stroked himself in long and slow movements. If he moved closer, he could see her from a better vantage, see her fingers plunging in and out of her, see the delicate pink—

A branch snapped under his foot.

Foolish fucking firewood, he cursed at himself. He was an ancient god of wooded glens and shadowed glades, in complete control of the forests in all their fashions... and he'd given himself away by stepping on a dry twig like a bumbling buffoon.

She snatched her hand from between her legs and scanned the forest. He held his breath again, cock still firmly in his grip, and remained motionless. Her eyes passed over him, and he waited for her to resume.

Instead, she took off into the woods at a full run.

The game began in earnest now. No more patience, no more careful stalking. Pure pursuit, raw and primal and utterly without mercy. He crashed through the undergrowth behind her, letting branches snap under his weight, letting her hear exactly what chased her through the darkness.

Hunt. Catch. Claim.

His body sang with predatory joy as he closed the distance. She stumbled, caught herself, then kept running. *Well done, little bunny. Make it challenging. Make the capture mean something when it finally comes.*

But even the surrounding forest felt impatient for her capture as a root caught her ankle. She went down hard, palms hitting earth, and he was there before she could roll away, crouched on the ground next to her. She was close enough to touch, close enough to smell the musk of her terror-sweat and the sharper scent of her musk.

She looked up at him and… grinned?

The expression caught him off guard. Not the fear he'd expected, not the desperate pleading most prey offered in their final moments before being either killed or claimed. This was pure, unashamed hunger. She *wanted* this. She had orchestrated her own capture, signed contracts, and paid whatever price Asmodeus set to lie beneath him in forest loam.

His form shifted without his own conscious thought. His bark peeled back and fell away to reveal soft, supple, dark skin beneath, his ligaments shortening ever so slightly, still tall but no longer towering. The moss and leaves that served as his tangle of hair and beard fell from his head and face, leaving him clean-shaven with a head of soft, dark stubble. His body was sculpted for pure pleasure. He hadn't even realized he was shifting into a human until it was over.

She reached up and grabbed his wrist. Her voice came out husky, demanding. "You caught me. What will you do to me now?"

Fuck.

The word exploded through his mind with volcanic force. Centuries, if not millennia, of clinical detachment shattered in an instant. This wasn't simply another contract anymore. This was *want*. This was *need*. His body responded as much to her nearly naked beauty as it did to her bare-naked hunger, her raw desire to be taken and ravaged.

A look of alarm spread across her face as she glanced down at his fully erect cock. She let out a sound that could have been a whimper or a moan; it drove him even madder with desire.

He revealed a predator's smile while looking down at her. "What will I do to you?" he asked as he leaned close to whisper in her ear. "Whatever I damn well please."

Chapter Four

Chase

*S**weet mother of God*, Celia thought when she first saw the leshy. He stepped from the forest to stand before her in the moonlight, and it was as if he'd stepped out from her very dreams.

Eight feet of raw, primal power emerged from the shadows. He was sculpted from the forest itself, his body carved with the raw perfection of a deity. His chest and abdominals rippled with muscle beneath bark-skin. Amid a thick mane of autumnal leaves, black antlers sprouted from his head like a dark king's crown. Thick intertwined branches twisted together to form his arms, powerful-looking limbs that seemed coiled with strength.

Once she saw him, his presence pulled at something primal deep within her. He was wilderness and freedom personified: untamed, dangerous, magnificent. Nature's perfect predator and protector wrapped in a package that stirred heat low in her belly and pooled between her legs.

But it was his eyes that stole her breath. Green fire burned in sockets too human for the beast he appeared to be, too intelligent, too knowing. They fixed on her with laser focus, and she felt exposed down to her soul.

He didn't move. Just watched her from ten feet away, letting her drink in the sight of him. Letting her decide whether to run or surrender.

Run. Her body chose before her mind could interfere.

She bolted for the trees. She didn't hear the sounds of pursuit... not yet. He was letting her flee. Letting her feel the illusion of escape before he decided the game had gone on long enough.

The forest swallowed her again, fog curling around her legs as she stumbled between ancient trunks. Her lungs burned with exertion and arousal, each breath sharp with cold air and wild need. She felt him back there, following at his own pace. Confident. Patient.

Inevitable.

A fallen log blocked her path. She vaulted over it and pressed herself against the massive oak beyond, bark rough against her back through thin silk. Her slip had torn more during her flight; the left shoulder hung in tatters, exposing the curve of her breast to moonlight.

Only the sounds of her panicked breathing broke the silence. *Where is he?*

She strained to listen and felt her desire mounting. The not-knowing was as intoxicating as the hunt itself. He could be anywhere. Watching from the shadows. Circling like a predator, planning how he'd take her when he finally tired of the game.

Her hand drifted down her body, fingertips skimming over silk dampened with perspiration. Lower, to where the fabric clung to curves slick with want. She was already so wet, so ready for him to claim her.

The bark of the ancient oak dug into Celia's back, but she barely noticed. Her focus was entirely consumed by the relentless pulse between her legs, a primal beat that demanded her attention. Her fingers, trembling with excitement, fear, and anticipation, slid below her navel, slid past her waist, slid down further.

She was slick and swollen, her arousal coating her thighs. Celia's fingertips brushed her clit, a gentle teasing that sent sparks up her spine and made her breath catch. The forest seemed to hold its breath with her, as if even the trees leaned in to watch her.

She threw her head back and bit her lip to suppress a moan. She rutted against the tree; the bark pulling her hair, and she wished it were him behind her; his long fingers entwined in her hair, pulling her against him.

She knew he was closing the distance. He was hunting her. She had to stay quiet, even though the thought of him catching her, taking her, brought a moan to her lips.

So close! I just want—

Her mind painted vivid images of her leshy with his ebony antlers and blazing green eyes. She imagined his massive hands wrapping around her, grasping her in an iron grip, fingers digging into her hard enough to bruise, the thickness of him—

A branch cracked to her left.

She jerked her hand away and held her breath. Nothing but fog and shadows, but she felt his presence like electricity in the air. Close. So close, she smelled the earthy scent of him.

Run. Now. The certainty hit her like lightning.

She pushed off the tree and ran.

He let her take five more steps before the forest erupted behind her.

Branches snapped like rifle shots as his massive form burst through the trees. He crashed through the underbrush with shocking speed. No more patient stalking. This was raw pursuit, primal and unrelenting.

Her feet flew over moss and leaves, guided by moonlight and instinct. Behind her, the sound of his approach grew louder. Closer. She could hear his breathing now, deep and controlled despite his speed.

He is toying with you. He could have caught you a dozen times already.

The knowledge sent fire racing through her veins. She was prey, but willing prey. Running because the chase fed something dark and hungry in both of them.

A root caught her ankle.

She fell hard, palms scraping against earth and stone. Before she could roll away, his massive form landed beside her in a crouch that shook the ground.

Up close, he was even more magnificent. Moonlight carved shadows along the planes of his chest, highlighting the predatory grace in every line of his body. His antlers drank in the moonlight, giving off the slightest gleam as he leaned over her, caging her against the forest floor.

Celia looked up into those emerald eyes and grinned.

The leshy's features began to shift. His bark clattered to the forest floor in large chunks, revealing dark skin that appeared supple and soft. His wild mane of red and orange leaves browned, blackened, curled, then drifted away, leaving behind a carpet of dark stubble. Nearly everything that marked him as a leshy faded or changed to fit her needs except his glowing green eyes...

And his polished ebony antlers.

The man who knelt above her was beautiful and dangerous. His face belonged on museum marble: sharp cheekbones, full mouth, eyes that burned with animal need rather than civilized hunger. But the power of the leshy remained, coiled in muscles that could break her or worship her with equal ease.

Part of her still wanted to run, didn't want the delicious chase to end, and she was about to scramble backwards away from him when she looked down between his legs.

He crouched there, looming over her, his cock already fully erect as he drank in the sight of her. *Good fucking God.* Despite herself, she whimpered at the thought of his girth stretching her, her eyes widening at the fear of the pain as well as the anticipation of the pleasure.

Celia reached up and grabbed his wrist, her fingers barely spanning the width of it. Her voice came out husky with need. "You caught me. What will you do to me now?"

His smile was predator and lover combined. "What will I do to you?" he asked. He leaned in close, and the earthy cedar scent of him made her mouth water with desire and anticipation as he whispered in her ear, "Whatever I damn well please."

Celia's heart pounded, the thrill of the chase still coursing through her veins. Her back arched as he pinned her to the forest floor, his body a furnace against hers. His cedar scent wrapped around her like a spell. His minty breath was hot on her neck as his teeth grazed the sensitive skin below her ear, trailing kisses down. She lay, breathless and exhilarated, beneath the leshy. She shivered, not from cold, but from the raw, primal need coursing through her veins.

"Oh God," she gasped, the word torn from her throat. Her hands clawed at the dirt, nails digging into soft earth as she writhed beneath him. The tattered remains of her slip did nothing to shield her from the night air or the heat of his touch.

He growled low in his throat, a sound that vibrated through her chest and settled between her thighs. His hands were rough, demanding, as they roamed her body, mapping every curve and hollow. She felt the hard length of him pressed against her hip, promises of pleasure and pain intertwined.

"Please," she whispered, a hollow plea. She knew the terms of her contract. This was part of her need, part of her urge. To be taken. To be used.

"I beg you," she whimpered, a nearly silent sound. Her legs parted, inviting him in, her slit drenched and ready. *Fuck me*, roared through her mind. She held her breath as she waited for him to enter.

He smiled as he pulled away from her and stood.

No, no, no. She shattered as he withdrew, confused, hurt, and cold from his sudden absence. His smile was wicked, and she thought he was simply enjoying the cruelty of watching her despair before she felt something snake around her ankles.

Vines slithered from the ground beneath her as branches dipped down from the canopy above. The leshy watched as her ankles and wrists were entwined before she was hoisted into the air. Vines coiled up her legs, pulling her thighs apart, as the branches wove together and formed a seat of soft leaves to cushion her ass. The branches swayed, bending to the leshy's will, creating a living cradle around her. Suspended in the air, she was at his mercy, and the realization sent a wave of heat through her.

Mother nature's sex swing, Celia thought with a delirious laugh as the vines tightened around her wrists.

The leshy approached. With his fingertips, he traced the arch of her cheek, the line of her jaw, and then the curve of her neck. His touch was hot and electric, sending jolts of pleasure through her. She leaned into his touch, a silent plea for more.

"You're mine now," he murmured, his voice a low growl that resonated through her, unearthly in its allure.

"Please," she begged for what seemed like the hundredth time.

"Please... what?" His tone was amused. His glowing green eyes burned into her.

"Please fuck me," she breathed.

"I plan to... mercilessly," he said as he inched closer to her.

She felt the tip of his cock pressed against her entrance. She swung her hips towards him, tugging against the vines, desperate to feel him inside of her.

"But not yet," he said as he took a step back.

He waved a hand, and the vines slid and danced across her skin. He kept his eyes locked on hers as the vines twerked and tweaked her nipples with a delicate and rhythmic precision. She squirmed and gasped in her swing.

Each touch sent a jolt of pleasure through her, a sensation that was both intense and infuriating. She arched her back, pressing into the vines, craving more. Through half-lidded eyes, she saw him watching her as his vines explored her body. There was a look of pleasure painted on his face.

Dear God, why do I feel so liberated when he watches?

With a subtle gesture from the leshy, the branches lifted her higher and spread her legs further apart. She was now looking down at him as he walked forward, his face between her thighs. She could almost reach out and touch his antlers were it not for the vines.

He leaned in, his breath hot against her swollen clit, as he slid his warm hands underneath her ass. "I must know," he murmured, "do you taste as delicious as your scent?"

Then his tongue flicked out, deft and hungry against her.

A moan escaped her, a sound of need that echoed through the forest. He was skilled, his tongue dancing over her clit, circling, teasing, before plunging deep inside her. He probed and plumbed her depths, his tongue making her feel so full, and she bucked her hips and swung against his mouth. A primal growl vibrated against her as he pulled her against him, his tongue and lips working furiously against her. The sensation was overwhelming, an intoxicating mix of pleasure and intensity that set her quivering.

The vines continued their dance, tweaking her nipples. They wrapped around her clit, pulsing in rhythm with his tongue, sending ripples of ecstasy cascading through her. She writhed in the vines as her moans filled the air.

His tongue was relentless, probing her deeply, exploring every inch of her. He knew exactly how to touch her, how to bring her to the brink and keep her there, suspended in a state of ecstasy. The vines tightened around her nipples, on the cusp of pain.

The leshy's tongue danced over her clit, circling, teasing, before plunging deep inside her again. The vines pulsed once more, matching the rhythm of his tongue, driving her closer to the edge.

Close, close, close.

He looked up at her, his glowing green eyes burning with desire. "Let go," he murmured, his voice a command she couldn't refuse.

She did.

Her orgasm ripped through her, a tsunami of rapture that set her shaking. The vines and branches tightened around her, holding her securely as she rode wave after wave of ecstasy. His tongue continued its dance, prolonging her pleasure, drawing out every last shiver as she drenched his face.

As her orgasm began to taper off, she leaned forward, vines loose enough for her to reach down, and grabbed the leshy's antlers to steady herself. The sound of him taking a startled breath preceded his guttural moan.

"Stop," he whispered, "those are sensitive."

Oh, are they?

She squeezed his antlers and pulled his head back to look into his otherworldly eyes, her arousal gleaming on his lips. "You said earlier," she squeezed harder, eliciting a satisfying moan from him, "something about fucking me mercilessly?"

With barely a second of delay, the vines dropped her down while splaying her legs apart. She was beyond soaked as he slammed himself into her, filling her with a single savage thrust, her cunt squelching obscenely around his girth.

Her cry echoed through the forest, a symphony of surrender and desire. He swung her back and forth with hard, relentless strokes, each one driving deeper into her. She felt impossibly full with him, as every inward thrust slammed into her cervix and sent ripples of euphoric pain throughout her body. The world narrowed to the point where their bodies joined; the slide of their sweat-slicked skin, her hands reaching up to grasp his antlers, his cock thrusting in and out of her.

"More," she demanded, surprising herself. Her fantasy had been to struggle, to fight, to be taken. She had originally envisioned clawing and biting the leshy to try to break away and continue the chase.

However, in the intense savagery of his fucking, in the masterful and fluid sway of the vines that held her, in the otherworldly way he pounded into her, she lost all desire to flee.

You have never *been fucked like this.*

"Harder," her voice was hoarse with need. She was leveraging herself against the vines by pulling and pushing his antlers, each swing down and forward to meet his brutal upward thrusts.

She squeezed his antlers, urging him deeper, faster. He moaned and complied, his body a merciless machine designed for her pleasure. Their combined cries and moans were unrestrained and raw; a primal duet of being taken and of taking.

She felt him everywhere, consuming her, possessing her. His mouth found the pulse point at her neck, and he bit down. He was not gentle, just shy of breaking skin, and she screamed, the sound swallowed by the forest.

"Yes," she panted, her body shaking with each thrust. "Like that. Don't you dare stop."

His growl was approving, feral. He reached up, his fingers finding the tight bundle of nerves at her core, circling her clit with a precision that sent surges of bliss through her. Her orgasm hit her like a tidal wave, sweeping away thought, reason, everything but the raw, animal need that drove her as her vision swam.

He didn't stop, didn't slow, pounding into her through the crest of her climax and into the aftershocks that followed. Without faltering in his relentless rhythm and with one hand still between her legs and another now on her breast, his fingers set to teasing both nipple and clit.

Her body was no longer her own, but a vessel for sensation, a plaything for his pleasure and hers. Her second orgasm never fully ended before the third one slammed into her. When she came again, harder this time, her screams echoed through the woods in a feral release she'd never known before, never even thought possible.

When he finally slowed, she was boneless, spent, her body limp and sated. Her grip on his antlers was loose. *I must be dying*, she thought. It was the only explanation for what was transpiring between them. Never had she been able to orgasm this many times, even when it was just herself, and yet this leshy had played her like a finely tuned instrument.

He lazily waved his hand, and the branches lifted her to eye level with him. His look was questioning, as if unsure if she would continue.

Surely he's not worried? She lowered a hand to cup his face, the same one that held the silent rune, and brushed a thumb over his cheekbone. A soft smile played on her lips, a stark contrast to the wild abandon of moments before.

"You caught me," she whispered, her voice breathless with laughter and residual desire. "You earned it."

He held her gaze, studying her, before he leaned in, capturing her mouth in a kiss that was both tender and fierce. He tasted of mint and berries. His body was a furnace, his cock still hard, still needy, pressing against her once more as she melted into him.

She spread her legs, welcoming him back inside. This time, their joining was slower, sweeter, but no less intense. He moved with deliberate care, each stroke designed to wring every last drop of ecstasy from her. She wrapped her arms around his neck, pulling him closer, her breath hot against his ear.

"Yes," she whispered, her voice a soft echo of her earlier cries. "Like that. Just like that."

Whereas before the swing allowed them to effortlessly slam into one another without abandon, this time it was used to glide him into her: fluid and languid.

He took her with deep, measured thrusts, his body a promise of both pleasure and protection. She felt cherished, worshipped, every inch of her skin alive with sensation. Her hips swung to meet his, their bodies moving in sync, a dance as old as the forest around them.

He wrapped one massive arm around her waist and another under her ass. The vines and branches fell away, and he pulled her close to him, shoving as much of his cock into her as he could as he slammed into her cervix again. She yelped a cry of pained pleasure as he stood there, her hands grasping his antlers and her legs wrapped around his waist.

He lowered both hands to grab her by the ass and planted his feet firmly on the ground. She felt as if he had speared her, the way he effortlessly held her aloft while inside her.

He could hold you up without using his hands.

He slid her up and down his length, rocking back and forth, his fingers clutching her ass with bruising force. Her nipples rubbed against his chest, and she clutched his antlers, knowing it gave him pleasure, as he increased the tempo. She leaned her face towards his, their mouths crashing together in a desperate kiss that captured her moaning screams.

Another orgasm built slowly, but not just for her this time. She felt him grow even thicker within her as he hastened his thrusts. He lifted her along his length before slamming her down and ramming into her with a brutal force that brought tears to her eyes. She feared she would black out from the pain, her vision blurring, her screams a mix of lust and ache before her fourth orgasm sent her body into electric convulsions.

He followed her over the edge, his body tensing as he spilled inside her. She felt his cock pulse as he filled her, and a low groan tore from his throat. Through the crazed storm of her orgasm, she marveled at how he somehow stayed upright and continuously fucked into her with the same furious intensity throughout his own climax.

The aftershocks of her orgasm still racked her body as he slowed his thrusts, pulled her body tight against his, and stood there holding her in his arms in the forest. She buried her face in his neck, allowing herself to go rag doll limp against him, still savoring the feeling of him inside of her as each twitch of his cock sent another shiver of exquisite agony throughout her.

For a long while, they stayed that way, locked together, their hearts pounding in unison.

Eventually, he pulled himself out of her and lowered her to the ground. Celia laughed softly and rested her head against his chest. *My silent dark woodland prince.*

The forest seemed to sigh around them, the rustle of leaves and the distant call of night birds a lullaby after the storm. She felt content, sated, her body aching in all the right ways.

They lay there together for a time in silence.

Chapter Five

Además

The forest floor pressed against Lahs's shoulder blades, earth and moss cool beneath his skin. His chest rose and fell in measured breaths, though his heart still thundered from the encounter.

When was the last time?

That question circled through his mind like the sage smoke the *Volkhv* used to burn at his sanctuary. He couldn't remember allowing himself such complete surrender to pleasure; not with a mortal, not with *anyone*.

Her head rested on his chest, the weight of it foreign yet... satisfying. His hand moved of its own accord, fingers tracing lazy patterns across the curve of her spine. The contact sent aftershocks through his system, his body still humming with the memory of being inside her. Of spilling inside of her.

She is magnificent.

That thought struck him with unexpected force. Not just her body, though that had exceeded every expectation. And not only her alluring aroma, though he'd never known rosemary and vanilla could smell so irresistible. But it was also the raw hunger she'd displayed, and the fearless way she'd met his violence with her own desperate need. Most mortals cowered when faced with his true nature. She had demanded more.

The silence between them was only broken by the whisper of wind through branches and the distant hoot of an owl. Neither spoke. Words felt unnecessary, almost profane, after what they'd shared. Her breathing had evened, but he knew she wasn't sleeping. Her fingers moved against his ribs, small touches that betrayed her restlessness.

Then she shifted.

Her lips pressed against his sternum, soft and warm. A kiss so gentle it might have been accidental, if not for the way her mouth lingered, tasting the salt on his skin. His muscles tightened beneath her touch, anticipation coiling in his gut.

Another kiss, lower this time. Then another, lower. Her tongue darted out to trace the line between muscle and sinew, mapping his body with methodical precision. His cock stirred, already responding to her despite having just spent himself inside her.

"Insatiable creature."

The observation carried no judgment—only admiration. She chuckled as she kissed her way down his taut torso, her dark chestnut hair spilling across his abdomen like silk. Each press of her lips sent sparks of sensation racing through his nerve endings. By the time she reached his navel, he was fully hard again, his shaft pressing against the soft swell of her breasts.

She noticed, of course. A soft hum of approval vibrated against his skin as she adjusted her position, letting her nipples graze along his length. The contact was maddening: too light, too teasing. His hips bucked involuntarily, seeking more friction.

Her laughter was low and throaty. "Impatient, aren't we?"

Before he could respond, her mouth closed around the head of his cock.

The breath left his lungs in a sharp hiss. Heat engulfed him, wet and welcoming, as her tongue swirled around his crown. Her hands wrapped around his shaft, fingers barely meeting around his girth. She worked him with skillful precision, her mouth moving up and down while her hands twisted in counterpoint.

Where did a mortal, an academic, a cloistered professor no less, learn such splendid technique?

The thought fragmented as she took him deeper, her throat muscles contracting around his length. He knew he was large, and it was no small feat for her to take him in her mouth, yet she somehow managed to. Stars burst behind his eyelids. She pulled back with deliberate slowness, her tongue tracing the thick vein that ran along his underside.

His hand fisted in her hair, not to guide but to anchor himself against the tide of sensation threatening to sweep him away. She moaned around him; the vibration sending shivers of euphoria straight to his core. Her mouth was relentless, alternating between deep, throat-conquering plunges and teasing licks that left him gasping.

The familiar tightness began building in his balls, pleasure coiling tighter with each bob of her head. His breathing grew ragged, his control slipping. Just a little more, and he would—

She stopped.

His eyes snapped open as cool air replaced the heat of her mouth. She was already moving, rising to her feet with fluid grace. Moonlight painted silver highlights across her naked form as she grinned down at him, pink lips swollen and glistening.

"I'm not finished running," she said as she spun and darted into the trees.

If his desire for release had been a fire before, her words forged it into a raging inferno.

Her laughter echoed through the forest as branches swallowed her pale form and she shouted, "Come catch me again if you can!"

A growl tore from his throat, primal and furious. The sound reverberated through the clearing, sending smaller creatures scurrying for cover. *Infuriating woman*. She had brought him to the very edge of climax, then fled like some woodland sprite. *No... like the bunny I named her for.* His cock throbbed with unfulfilled need, every nerve screaming for release.

"Running through *my* forest, little bunny?" He surged to his feet, muscles bunching as his form began to shift. "Run, little bunny, run. Scamper off through the brush."

His skin thickened into bark, a tangle of autumn leaves burst forth among his antlers, as his other supernatural aspects reasserted themselves: enhanced senses, ligaments elongating into bark, predatory grace, the single-minded focus of a hunter denied his prize. Her scent hung in the air like a challenge, marking her passage through the undergrowth. "Hide, if you like. It will make no difference." He knew she heard his fury-laced words when her giggle filtered through the trees.

This time, he would not toy with her. *This* time, he would take what was his to claim.

The chase was brief and brutal. Where before he had allowed her the illusion of escape, now he pursued with deadly efficiency. He crashed through the forest like an avalanche, branches snapping beneath his weight. Her laughter had turned breathless, tinged with genuine excitement as she realized the change in his demeanor.

He caught her beside a fallen log, his thick arm encircling her waist and lifting her from her feet. She gasped, her back pressed against his bark-skin torso. Without ceremony, he bent her over the moss-covered trunk, his hand between her shoulder blades, holding her in place.

"You want to run?" His voice was like the rumbling thunder before a storm. "You want to tease?"

His other hand found the rune on her wrist, fingers hovering just above the pale mark. One flicker of light, one sign that she wanted this to end, and he would release her immediately. The rune remained dark.

"You *want* this," he gritted out. "You *want* me to take you like an animal?"

He shifted back, his bark replaced by warm, soft skin as he molded to her size. He positioned himself at her entrance, sliding his hands to her hips, cock teasing her... but not entering. She braced herself on her elbows, ass lifted in offering, as she silently begged for him to take her.

Fury battled with desire as he watched her shake her ass and push her drenched slit back towards him. He drank in the sight of her swollen lips quivering against the tip of his head.

"Such a needy little slit." Then he entered her slowly from behind, the head of his cock sliding through her tight wetness, his grip on her hips bruising. She was soaked, her body betraying how much the chase had aroused her.

"Be good," he admonished as he thrust forward, filling her in one savage stroke, "and let me in."

She whimpered, an impatient cry, as he struggled for control, enjoying the way she squeezed around him.

"You *craved* this, didn't you, little bunny?" His voice shook partly from rage and the intense tightness of her cunt.

"Yes!" Her cry split the night: part shock, part pleasure, entirely wanton.

"Then fucking take it." He set a punishing pace, his hips slamming against her ass with each thrust, balls hitting her clit, eliciting a groan from both of them. The sound of flesh meeting flesh echoed through the trees, accompanied by her breathless moans and his own guttural grunts.

She pushed back against him, meeting his violence with her own ravenous hunger. Her hands clutched the bark of the fallen tree, knuckles white with the force of her grip. He saw the delicate curve of her neck, the way her hair spilled across her shoulders like liquid shadow.

"Yes," she gasped, the word torn from her throat. "Like that. Don't stop."

As if he could. His body moved with mechanical precision, driven by a need so intense it bordered on madness. She had reduced him to his most basic components: hunger, desire, the primal urge to claim and possess.

His hand left her hip to tangle in her silky hair, pulling her head up so he could see her face. Her hazel eyes were wild, dark pupils blown wide with lust. Her delicious pink lips parted as she panted, small sounds of pleasure escaping with each breath.

Fuck she was gorgeous like this. The sight pushed him over the edge. His orgasm crashed over him, pleasure so intense it bordered on pain. He buried himself to the hilt as he spent himself inside her, his cry echoing through the forest and shaking the very trees.

She followed him over, her body convulsing around his cock as her own climax tore through her. They collapsed together onto the soft moss, limbs tangled and hearts racing.

For a long moment, neither moved. The forest held its breath around them. Lahs's arm tightened around her waist, pulling her closer against his chest. *What is she doing to me?* The question whispered through his mind as exhaustion fought to claim him.

I cannot believe a mortal matched my stamina.

Celia lay nestled against his chest. The forest canopy above them filtered moonlight into silver patterns across her skin. The scent of earth and moss surrounded them, mixed with the musk of their passion.

She shifted, tilting her head to look up at him with renewed energy. Her hazel eyes held a vulnerability that made something twist in his chest. *Like autumn's leaves*, he thought, memorized by their beauty as she stared at him.

"Are you," she stopped and bit her lower lip, "are you real? I mean, *truly* real? Or are you just part of the fantasy?"

Lahs threw back his head and laughed, a rich sound that echoed through the trees. The very branches seemed to sway with his mirth. "Real?" He cupped her face gently, thumb brushing across her cheekbone. "Little bunny, I have walked the forests of the world since before your ancestors learned to make fire. I have watched empires rise and fall like the changing of the seasons." He leaned forward and pressed a kiss onto her forehead. "Besides, reality is not what mortals think it is. You are dreaming, yes, but you are also awake. Both can be true."

She frowned as she said, "That is very... cryptic."

"The best truths usually are." His antlers caught the moonlight as he shifted to face her more fully.

"What should I call you?" Celia asked.

"By my name," he said with a wry smile.

That elicited a timid laugh, like the chirping of a tiny bird. "Fair enough. What is your name, then?"

He paused. *Dare I grace her with the truth of my own name?* The hesitation was born from centuries, if not millennia, of holding himself apart and above the mere mortals beneath him.

And yet...

There was something about *this* mortal. Some ethereal and indescribable feeling about her that he struggled against—that he was losing to. It was this incomprehensible feeling that compelled him to lean close to her, gaze into her mesmerizing eyes, and breathe his name. "Lahs."

She inhaled, held her breath, then exhaled as she reached up to touch his face. She repeated his name over and over again, as if she were tasting the sound of it, savoring the feel of it on her tongue. "It's a beautiful name," she whispered.

"It gladdens my heart that you approve," he said. "But, tell me something, little bunny. Of all the creatures from myths and legends, why did you choose a leshy? Why not some beautiful fae prince or noble centaur to be your hunter?"

Celia's cheeks flushed, but she met his gaze. "Because you are," she paused, searching for words, "you are the physical manifestation of everything I have denied myself. The wild, untamed parts of nature that civilization teaches us to fear. You are freedom incarnate; the whisper of wind through ancient trees, the call of something primal that exists beyond rules and expectations. A sentient force of the wilderness that reminds us we are still animals beneath our carefully constructed civilized manners."

Her voice grew softer, then more reverent. "You represent the part of myself I have caged behind books and theories and proper behavior. The part that wants to run barefoot through moonlit forests and feel earth beneath my skin and remember what it means to be gloriously, unapologetically alive."

Lahs stared at her, wordless. His chest ached. In all his centuries, mortals had often sought him out, but always *for* something. To spare their villages from blight, to bless their harvests, to grant them power or protection. They came with offerings and trembling knees, motivated by fear or greed or desperation.

But this remarkable woman had come to him out of pure desire. Not for what he could *give* her, but for what he *was*. The distinction struck him like lightning.

"You see me," he murmured, wonder threading through his voice.

Celia looked away, suddenly shy again. Her fingers plucked at the moss beneath them. "Will I—" she swallowed hard as she composed her thoughts. "After tonight ends, after this fantasy concludes... will I ever see you again?"

Gone was her confidence as the question jolted him like a second strike of lightning. Lahs caught her shoulders, turning her to face him fully. He wanted her to understand just how remarkable she truly was. His radiant green eyes burned with an intensity that made her breath catch.

"Listen to me," he said, his voice rough. "I want to watch you discover your wildness in a hundred different forests. I want to see you laugh under summer storms and dance in winter snows. I want to share every sunrise that paints your skin tawny, every sunset that makes your eyes gleam like emeralds and gold. I want to take you under the light of every full moon when the world feels electric with possibility, and during every new moon when the darkness holds infinite promise."

She held her breath, and her eyes shimmered with tears, but she was silent. Lahs tightened his grip as he continued.

"Little bunny, the mountains would crumble and the seas would boil before anything could keep me from you. I would set all the forests of the world *on fire* if it meant seeing your face again."

His forehead pressed against hers, and he whispered, "I have existed for millennia without this... this *feeling* you have gifted me. You've awakened something within me I didn't know I wanted, didn't know I needed."

Two tears streamed down Celia's cheeks. "But how? I am nothing special. I am just... *me*. And this is just a fantasy."

"Nothing about this is *just* anything," Lahs said fiercely.

He kissed her then, soft and reverent, tasting salt from her tears. When he pulled back, his eyes held promises that seemed to span eternity.

"This is not an ending," he whispered against her lips. "This is barely a beginning."

He kissed her more deeply then, tasting her as he held her against him. She slid so perfectly into his embrace, as if they were carved to fit together. He could have grown roots and never moved from that spot again as long as she stayed with him.

She pulled away, rising to her feet, and looked down at him with her lovely, wide eyes. "Will you chase me again?"

Whatever this had started as, he was no longer certain who was the hunter and who was the prey. As he stood, he pressed his lips against her throat and replied, "Always. Now run, my little bunny."

Chapter Six

Payment

The bed felt like liquid silk beneath Celia's body; lotus silk sheets that whispered against her skin with every subtle movement. She smelled the faint trace of amber and cedar in the air, luxurious scents that matched the opulent chamber she'd awakened in. Where was this room? She couldn't remember walking through the door, couldn't remember leaving the forest at all.

Her body felt different. Alive. Every nerve ending hummed with residual pleasure, her muscles loose and sated in ways she'd never experienced. When she shifted, she felt the tender ache between her thighs, the sweet soreness across her breasts where phantom teeth had marked her; evidence of what had transpired in those shadowed woods.

In the woods... with Lahs.

His name bloomed across her thoughts like heat spreading through her chest. *Lahs.* She rolled onto her side, pulling a pillow against her body, inhaling deeply as a smile lit her face. The lingering scent of earth and wild things clung to her skin beneath the rosewater someone had used to wash her.

Someone had washed her. Dressed her in this silk nightgown. Tucked her into this bed. *I don't remember any of that. What is the last thing I remember?*

Being chased through the woods again and again. Being caught again and again. Being taken again and again. Then... falling asleep curled against Lahs while feeling more safe and satiated than she ever had in her life. *That* was the last thing she remembered.

The practical part of her brain, the professor who analyzed and categorized everything, demanded that she question the logistics. Where had the forest gone? How had she gotten here? But that voice felt distant now, muffled beneath the roar of her pulse whenever she remembered the weight of Lahs's body, the scrape of his teeth, the way he'd looked at her as a starving man would stare at a feast.

"Now run, my little bunny," he'd growled against her throat.

And I had run. And he had caught me. Sweet mother of God, how he had caught me.

Her fingers traced the spot on her wrist where the emergency rune had glowed faintly all evening; faint, but never once bright enough to end her fantasy. She had checked it obsessively at first, needing the reassurance that escape existed as an option. But by the second chase, she'd forgotten it entirely.

She pressed her thighs together, feeling the echo of him still inside her. How could a leshy, a creature of bark and branch and primal hunger, make her feel more seen than any human lover she'd ever had? He'd read her body like a text written in a language specifically for him. He found every hidden desire she'd been too ashamed to voice aloud, then drew it out with hands that gentled when she trembled and roughened when she begged.

Because it wasn't just physical. The realization was as sudden and unexpected as a slap. She sat up, the sheets pooling around her waist.

He'd spoken to her between the hunts. Whispered things she couldn't dismiss as mere performance.

"You are exquisite when you surrender," he'd murmured against her temple, his thumb brushing away a tear she hadn't realized she'd shed. *"Not because you are weak. Because you are strong enough to let go."*

Words like that were not in the contract she'd signed. Asmodeus had not written that she was to be fawned over and flattered. Neither was the way Lahs had held her afterwards, his fingers threading through her hair in reverence, his minty breath matching the rhythm of hers until she'd stopped shaking. *That* certainly was not in the contract.

A leshy. A supernatural forest deity that had been paid or coerced to fulfill a fantasy. Her fantasy. That was all that had been expected of him.

What reason would he have to lie?

Celia pulled her knees to her chest, resting her chin there. Her reflection stared back from an ornate mirror across the room; a woman with wild chestnut hair and kiss-swollen lips, hazel eyes bright with something that looked dangerously close to hope.

She wasn't the same. She couldn't be. You didn't get chased through moonlit woods by a creature who fucked like worship and then walked away unchanged.

The question was whether she wanted to change back to who she'd been before the chase. Before Lahs.

The bruises were already fading, she noticed with an academic curiosity. Dark fingerprints on her hips grew lighter even as she watched. Some type of magic, then. The contract's protection extended beyond emotional safety into physical recovery. Clever. Practical. Something that she would have thought completely impossible twenty-four hours ago.

But her bone-deep satisfaction? *That* remained untouched. It radiated through her like warmth from a smoldering coal fire, deep and lasting and utterly transformative.

"*Palomita*, you look like a woman who has discovered something about herself."

Asmodeus's voice drew her attention to the doorway. He leaned against the frame, arms crossed, watching her with those knowing golden eyes. Had he been there long? The thought should have embarrassed her, lying spent and gloriously disheveled as she was, but embarrassment felt foreign now. Distant.

"I feel like one," she said, her voice carrying a new huskiness.

"How *else* are you feeling?" His voice carried his accented lilt, warm honey over silk. He walked to the nightstand near her bed and poured her a glass of water.

She accepted it, noting how the liquid seemed to shimmer. "Changed," she said simply, because it was the truth and her mind couldn't conjure an academic euphemism for metamorphosis and transformation.

"As you should." He settled into the chair across from her, one leg crossed over the other and his hands atop his knee, in a pose of casual elegance. "You are welcome back anytime, you know. Simply ask the bartender upstairs to speak with Damien, and I will find you."

Celia paused, the glass halfway to her lips. "Who is Damien?"

A slow smile spread across his perfect features, the kind that suggested he was enjoying a private joke. "I am, *pequeña profesora*. That is the name I give to mortals who frequent my establishment."

"But you introduced yourself to me as Asmodeus." The confusion must have been evident in her voice, because his smile widened.

"Because I *am* Asmodeus, Dr. Campbell. The Sin of Lust. Prince of the Second Circle." He gestured around them with casual authority. "But I do not bother introducing myself properly to most mortals. They would simply not understand. You, however..." His golden eyes fixed on hers with unsettling intensity. "With your background in occult studies, I knew you would comprehend who I am. *What* I am."

Celia set down her glass with deliberate care, her academic mind recoiling from the impossible claim. Earlier in the evening, she had assumed the man had taken on the name as an affectation, an eccentric stage name to woo and wow his clients.

"No," she said as she shook her head and frowned. " That's... no. Asmodeus is a literary construct, a symbolic representation of human carnality within theological discourse. The figure appears across multiple mythological traditions as an archetypal manifestation of forbidden desire, serving as an externalized projection of internal moral conflict. The anthropomorphization of abstract concepts such as lust into Asmodeus, Abaddon into Wrath, or Belphegor into sloth simply represents humanity's attempt to categorize and distance itself from uncomfortable aspects of human nature through the creation of supernatural scapegoats."

Asmodeus nodded as she spoke, a bemused expression on his face.

Her analytical brain kept firing off facts as it rationalized his claim away. She barely paused for breath, the familiar comfort of academic language flowing through her. "Modern psychological interpretation suggests these figures function as psychological tools for processing repressed 'sinful' impulses within restrictive religious frameworks. The persistence of such figures in literature from Milton to contemporary Gothic fiction demonstrates their continued utility as metaphorical devices rather than literal entities."

When she was finished, they sat in silence for a moment before he gave her a slow clap. Then he shrugged and waved a hand, the gesture somehow managing to be both elegant and dismissive. "Ah, *mi pequeña profesora*, your mind simply cannot wrap itself around too many reality-shattering revelations at once, can it? First, you discover that your deepest fantasies can be made manifest, then that leshies are more than creatures of myth. Now you must contend with the notion that the beings you have studied are not merely symbols scribbled in dusty tomes."

He leaned back and settled into his chair. "This reminds me of a delightful encounter I had with one Johann Weyer, the Dutch physician, back in the... sixteenth century? Brilliant man, truly. I called him *Vissig* as a little joke. He hated it," Asmodeus said with a chuckle. "When I had met him, the man had devoted his life to proving that demonic possession was nothing more than mental illness, that what people attributed to supernatural forces were simply manifestations of melancholia and hysteria."

His eyes took on a distant quality, as if he were watching the memory play out before him. "I found *Vissig* in his study in Düsseldorf, many years after he'd already written his famous tome '*De Praestigiis Daemonum*' refuting the existence of demons, witchcraft, and magic. He was so passionate about debunking what he saw as superstition, citing medical authorities, explaining how the human mind could manifest symptoms that ignorant people attributed to demons."

Celia found herself leaning forward despite her better judgment.

"When I appeared at *Vissig's* door, do you know what he did? He immediately began diagnosing himself. Spent twenty minutes explaining to me exactly why I was a visual hallucination brought on by too much stress and study and too little sleep. The poor man tried to cure his own 'delusion' with herbal remedies while I sat there watching." Asmodeus chuckled, the sound rich with genuine amusement. "I finally had to demonstrate some rather *convincing* supernatural abilities to persuade him that perhaps his theories, while admirably scientific, were not quite comprehensive enough to explain all phenomena."

His gaze returned to Celia with that knowing intensity. "The fascinating part, *palomita*, was what happened afterwards. Once he accepted that the supernatural did indeed exist alongside the medical explanations he championed, he became far more open-minded in his work. His later writings acknowledged that both possibilities could coexist: mental illness and genuine spiritual intervention."

"So you see, *mi pequeña profesora*, sometimes the most brilliant minds are the most resistant to new data when it contradicts their established worldview. But you have already taken the first step. You have moved from theory into practice, from studying desire to experiencing it. The rest is simply... intellectual adjustment."

"Intellectual adjustment?" She repeated his words with a thick slather of incredulousness. "Accepting that the Sin of Lust, and by extension his brothers—"

"And sisters," Asmodeus said as he raised a perfectly manicured finger.

"Yes, well... accepting that you, your brothers, and your sisters are all real flesh and blood is a bit more than a simple *adjustment.*"

The silence stretched between them, heavy with implications. Celia stared into her glass, watching the stillness of the water and wishing her mind could be that placid and tranquil. Her academic training warred with the evidence of her senses, with the lingering heat in her blood that whispered of impossibilities made real.

"Did he... did Weyer ever write about your encounter?" she asked finally, her voice barely above a whisper as she looked at him.

Asmodeus's eyes flashed a brilliant gold as his sharp-toothed smile widened. "Oh, yes! *Vissig* wrote his appendix to '*De Praestigiis Daemonum*' only a few years after our first encounter."

"You," Celia started, then stopped. "Were you the reason Weyer wrote '*Pseudomonarchia Daemonum*'later in his life?"

His laughter was both deep and warm, forcing the smallest smile to quirk at her lips. "I should not be so surprised that you would know *Vissig's* work," he said, "given your expertise and field of study. He learned that truth is far stranger and more beautiful than any theory we construct to contain it." Asmodeus's smile was gentle now, almost tender. "Much like you are learning, I suspect."

I could write an entire book on what I've learned in the past twenty-four hours.

Celia simply nodded, sipped her water, and let her mind sort through everything Asmodeus had told her.

He rose from the chair with fluid grace, then settled onto the edge of the bed. The mattress barely dipped under his weight. "You never used the rune. Not once."

Celia glanced at her wrist. The rune had returned to its dormant state, barely visible against her skin. "I didn't want to."

"I knew you would not want to, but it was there for your peace of mind, *pequeña profesora*. My Second Circle exists to satiate all desires, either known or hidden."

Heat bloomed on her cheeks. *Hidden desires, indeed.* She'd thought one chase would have been enough, yet she found her desire to be hunted only increased after her initial climax.

"The experience exceeded expectations," she said, falling back on academic language because the truth felt too raw to speak aloud. *But, heaven help me, I want to see Lahs again and again and again,* thinking back to his moving words.

"If that is the case, then it is time for my payment." Asmodeus reached toward her temple, his fingertips hovering just above her skin. "A memory, *palomita*. Just one."

She should have protested. Should have asked which one, demanded details, and negotiated terms. Instead, she felt something soft and warm bloom behind her eyes; a sensation like fingers trailing through her mind, gentle as silk scarves. The touch was intimate, more personal than any physical contact, and strangely... pleasant.

"There," he murmured, withdrawing his hand. "Beautiful. Thank you."

What did he take? A childhood memory of playing with her dolls and arranging elaborate chase scenarios? The first time she'd read a gothic romance and felt that strange flutter in her stomach when the heroine was carried off? Something else entirely? She searched her memories, but everything felt intact.

Did it even matter what memory he'd taken as payment? After all, was there anything she wouldn't give up for what she had just experienced? No, she knew with certainty, for *him,* it would be anything.

Which caused her to ask, "Will I remember what happened in the forest?"

"Every exquisite detail, of course." He rose to leave, then paused at the threshold. "Tell me, *pequeña profesora,* what comes next for a woman who has tasted her deepest desires?"

Celia stretched against the silk sheets, her body responding to the phantom memory of strong hands, reverent kisses, and desperate hunger that made her heart flutter and core tighten once more. *What comes next?* A return to her neat apartment, her ordered routine, her carefully compartmentalized life?

The thought felt absurd. *No, I* will *see Lahs again... and the hunt will begin anew.*

She smiled, slow and dangerously. "Next time, I think I want to be the one who chases."

Asmodeus's answering laugh was rich and warm. "Oh, Celia... you are going to be a delight."

The door closed with a whisper, leaving her alone with her thoughts and the lingering scent of cedar.

Celia closed her eyes and smiled.

Epilogue

Lahs did not enjoy being in his human form. He felt small, weak, and disconnected from the world around him; from the Earth he loved and tended. He especially did not enjoy it when he had to be around other mortals.

And there were *always* mortals in Oubliette, mingling unknowingly with those of his kind and others.

So, he admitted that it must have meant something significant that he found himself walking up the stairwell from the Second Circle, heading towards the crowded nightclub above. The thought of being bombarded by the fleshy stench of walking meat bags very nearly drove him back down the stairs, down the hall, through Second Circle's door, back to his forest.

But he persevered. Again. For the third time in as many weeks, he found himself making his way to Malacoda, the ever-present demon who served as the steward of Oubliette in Asmodeus's absence for this particular city. Lahs hoped the demon wouldn't be preoccupied, but doubted his luck; last week, he had to wait nearly an hour for Malacoda to resolve a dispute between some bickering patrons before he could approach.

Such is the life of a servant when the master is away.

As Lahs continued up the spiraling stairwell, he nearly bumped into the towering bulk of a boar-faced demon, his tusks glistening in the dim light.

"Pardon me, Ciriatto," Lahs said. He moved to one side of the stairwell to allow the massive member of the Malebranche to continue down the stairs.

The demon didn't move.

"Lord of Leaves and Father of Forests," Ciriatto said as he dipped his head. "Asmodeus requests you join him in his study."

Lahs cursed his root-rotted, leaf-blighted luck. "I was under the impression that the Prince of Lust was visiting his other Oubliette locations for a time?"

"He was," Ciriatto said. "And he will continue to do so. *After* he speaks with you."

Lahs knew that it would be pointless to attempt to talk his way out of this; Ciriatto could not be bribed nor lied to. And Lahs refused to lose dignity by attempting to flee the boar-faced demon.

"Lead the way," Lahs said.

It was a short walk to a pair of black iron doors. Ciriatto pushed one door open and gestured for Lahs to enter. Asmodeus's private study existed in perpetual dim light, with heavy mahogany panels drinking the light from scattered candles that never seemed to burn down. The air smelled of herbs and amber, thick enough to coat the throat with each breath. Behind a desk of carved ebony, Lahs found the Prince of Lust bent over an enormous tome, his attire immaculate in forest green and gold trim.

The ledger was the size of a dining table, bound in midnight-black leather that seemed to shift and breathe under candlelight. Asmodeus wrote in it with methodical precision, his elegant script flowing across pages that appeared to document contracts. Lahs imagined how every fantasy and every whispered desire that passed through the doors of the Second Circle must have been kept within that journal.

Obsessive record-keeping, Lahs thought, though he understood the necessity. The Second Circle operated on contracts. Contracts required documentation. Still, watching the Prince of Lust hunched over paperwork like some celestial accountant struck him as absurd.

"Sit," Asmodeus said without lifting his gaze from the page. His quill, carved from what looked like bone, scratched against parchment with the rhythm of rain on stone.

Lahs dropped into the leather chair across from the desk. The seat molded itself to his frame, recognizing his specific weight and heat signature. Everything in this room adapted to its occupants. Everything served the Prince's comfort and control.

"The Campbell contract concluded successfully." Asmodeus finally set down his quill, those impossibly golden eyes fixing on Lahs with laser focus. "No complications. No use of the emergency protocols. Client satisfaction appears to have been exceptional."

The careful neutrality in Asmodeus's voice made Lahs's jaw tighten. "The mortal received exactly what she contracted for. Nothing more."

"Mmm." Asmodeus leaned back in his chair, fingers steepled beneath his chin. "And your assessment of her performance?"

Performance. As if the woman had been acting instead of writhing beneath him with genuine hunger, her nails scoring his back while she gasped.

"Nothing more than another bag of meat desperate to experience what she was unable to pursue in her mundane existence," Lahs said, trying to sound indifferent, careful to not reveal the blossoming of affection for the mortal. To owe a favor to a friend was one thing, but to give a demon your weakness was another.

Asmodeus's smile sharpened at the corners. "Perhaps. Yet her rune remained inactive throughout, *Les Pravedniy.* Even after you became... *enthusiastic.*"

Heat flared beneath Lahs's skin, and he was again reminded how much he hated being in human form.

The memory of Celia's body yielding beneath his, her throat bared in surrender, flashed through his mind. How she'd laughed when he'd caught her the second time, not in fear but in triumph, as if she'd won their game.

"She wanted to be taken roughly," Lahs said. "The contract specified—"

"I know what the contract specified. I wrote it." Asmodeus tilted his head, studying Lahs. "What I find curious is your continued focus on this particular client."

Lahs's muscles locked. Had his thoughts been so transparent? "I have no focus, old friend."

"And yet, *mi corazón de roble*, your very presence here in my club—uninvited and unexpected—speaks otherwise."

Lahs bristled, feeling embarrassed at being caught at his fledgling attempt at subterfuge. "I was unaware that I *required* an invitation. I would have thought our friendship—a friendship that has endured the rise and fall of empires—would transcend the need for something as frivolous as *invitations*."

"Lahs," Asmodeus said as he patted the air between them, "you are welcome at any of my Oubliettes at any time and you always have been, for as long as there have been Oubliettes. However," he said with a shrug, "you have visited this *specific* location more in the past few weeks than you have *ever* stepped foot inside any Oubliettes. Ever."

Lahs stood as silent as his brother trees, wishing he were back in his forest.

"Add to that," Asmodeus continued as a grin crept across his face, "that you have asked Malacoda if he's seen the good Dr. Campbell since your encounter?"

Still, Lahs was silent.

"Twice you have asked, *mi corazón de roble*."

Damn him. Nothing escaped the Prince's notice within his walls.

"Simple curiosity," Lahs lied. "Her lack of fear was highly... unusual for a meat bag."

What he couldn't admit was how her wild laughter haunted him. How the memory of her warmth lingered on his skin like a brand, refusing to fade with time as all mortal encounters should. How the thoughts of her set his blood-sap afire. Admitting any of that aloud meant Asmodeus had him by the balls, for she was only mortal and he was not.

The knowing grin was still on Asmodeus's face as he said, "Well, I admire that level of *professional curiosity* you have discovered."

The casual emphasis made Lahs want to bare his teeth; a surprising and animalistic behavior. The Prince of Lust's ability to inject meaning into the most minor inflection was legendary, and right now that skill was focused entirely on dissecting Lahs's reactions.

He knows.

Of course, he knew. Asmodeus could read desire like other demons read contracts: with unerring, infuriating accuracy.

"Will that be all?" Lahs started to turn, but Asmodeus raised one perfectly manicured finger.

"Actually, no. Professor Campbell has requested a follow-up appointment. Next month, I believe. Something about wanting to explore the *predator* role herself." The Prince's eyes glittered with malicious amusement. "Naturally, I'll need someone to serve as prey. Someone with the stamina to provide an adequate challenge."

Lahs's heart slammed against his ribs like a caged animal. The thought of her hunting him, of those clever hands binding him while she took what she wanted?

Fuck.

His cock stirred traitorously, and from Asmodeus's widening smile, his reaction hadn't gone unnoticed.

"I am sure either you or Ciriatto will find a suitable partner for her," Lahs managed.

"*Mi corazón de roble*," Asmodeus said as he rose from his chair, walked around his desk, and reached up to cup Lahs's face. The Prince's long, slender fingers radiated heat against Lahs's skin, as if he were an inferno made manifest. "You see, Professor Campbell specifically requested *you*." Asmodeus looked up, predatory and pleased. "It seems you made quite an impression during your convincing performance with her."

The words burned into him. She'd asked for him specifically. Not just anybody, not just *another* leshy. Him. The knowledge sent liquid fire racing through his veins, and he had to force his breathing to remain steady. He refused to show how much the revelation affected him, but it did. She had not lied. She wanted *him*.

"If that's what the contract requires," he said.

"It is." Asmodeus withdrew his hot hands and made his way back to his chair. "Though I suspect next time will prove far more *intense* than her initial exploration." Asmodeus picked up his quill again, clearly dismissing him. "I trust you'll prepare accordingly."

Lahs stood, eager to escape before the Prince could probe deeper into reactions he barely understood himself. He'd made it to the door when curiosity overrode self-preservation.

"Her payment," Lahs said, remembering the terms of the contract. "What memory did you take?"

The scratching of the quill on parchment stopped. In the sudden silence, Lahs heard his own heartbeat, heard the distant moans and screams of clients on the floor above.

"Dear Lahs," Asmodeus said, voice warm with genuine affection and something darker. "I took the memory I desired most."

The non-answer was classic Asmodeus: revealing nothing while implying everything. Lahs's hands flexed at his sides. What memory could the Prince of Lust possibly desire from a mortal academic? Her earliest fantasy? Some childhood trauma that shaped her desires? Or something else entirely?

"Good evening," Asmodeus added with finality.

Lahs pushed through the heavy door and into the corridors beyond, his mind churning with questions he couldn't ask and desires he could only fulfill with her. Behind him, the soft scratch of quill on parchment resumed, documenting secrets and contracts in that endless ledger.

Next month. Four weeks to prepare for a woman who wanted to hunt him, to claim him, to turn their dynamic inside out. Four weeks to convince himself this was just another favor for an old friend, that she was nothing more than another bag of meat.

Four weeks to lie to himself about the anticipation already building in his chest like a second heartbeat.

The stairwell back down to the Second Circle stretched before him, familiar and comforting. But tonight, even the stone halls of Oubliette felt different. Tonight, everything smelled of rosemary and vanilla as the demon's domain responded to his desires.

Fuck.

Thank you, my beloved chaos *lectores*, for picking up this book and taking the leap of faith to check out an indie author. It really means the world to me. I truly hope Captured Prey gave you a much needed darkly delicious escape despite how short it was. And just so we're clear...there is *so much more* where that came from. The love poured into world building is equally important and with each story, a little more is revealed in the symbiotic relationship of the mortals and supernaturals while gods play mafia in the background intent to rule through the currency of worshippers.

I do want to give a fair warning, though: my catalog is a wild ride in the best possible way. I write across a broad spectrum of romance, from completely unhinged monster smut to sweeping dark romantasy epics with a sprinkling of contemporary. The common thread? High heat, powerful emotions, unapologetic morals, and happily-ever-afters every time.

I aim, in each book, to explore kink, desire, and the complexities of love for characters thirty-five and older (when I can!). However, I do have a soft spot for full-body tattoos and tragic villains which may come across in my writings as I research folklore and myths.

If you'd like to continue our relationship —because consent is key—along with gaining access to bonus smut, spicy artwork, and info on my other projects, come find me at www.renormist.com.

Additionally, Newsletter subscribers get first access to:
• free bonus content

• spicy art drops

• early updates

• exclusive Second Circle request forms where each quarter, I pull one subscriber's prompt and write a custom short story.

And lastly, your TBR is probably overflowing (same), but if you're not sure what to pick up next, here are a few options:

★ Dark Romantasy – Heretical Gods Series

Fated Rebirth , A Dark Fantasy Romance delivers grim-dark mythic romantasy with vengeance, divine rebellion, and a mafia-coded pantheon. If you love found family, frenemies-to-lovers tension, morally grey demons, and high-stakes emotional payoff, this one is for you. And yes, Asmodeus will make his appearance.

★ Dark Contemporary – Star-Cross'd Fates Series

One More Chance is an emotional, second-chance marriage-in-crisis romance told entirely from a deeply flawed but redeemable male POV. A story of betrayal, regret, and the brutal climb toward forgiveness when love tries to survive the damage of the past. Here, you are given a glimpses of how one god's choice led to mortals' souls being trifled with and how those mortals move forward given a chance to fix their mistakes in a contemporary setting. Audible available as well!

Before We Belong is a slow-burn, why-choose contemporary romance that explores redemption, vulnerability, and the courage to redefine what love and belonging can look like. Perfect for readers who crave emotional depth, found family, and forbidden love threaded with sensuality and heart.

*Coming soon! Subscribe to my newsletter to get access when it drops for Pre-Order

Once again, thank you again for taking this adventure with me. I hope we meet again between the pages soon.

Books by Reno R. Mist

Star-Cross'd Fates Series
One More Chance, A Redemption Novel*
Before We Belong*

Heretical Gods Series
Fated Rebirth, A Dark Fantasy Romance

A Second Circle Entry Series
Captured Prey, A Primal Play Novella*

For those interested in a custom short story with Second Circle, sign up for my newsletter Newsletter Sign Up

*These stories can be read as standalones

www.ingramcontent.com/pod-product-compliance
Lightning Source LLC
Chambersburg PA
CBHW070014140726
47908CB00020B/1396